You, Me and Empathy

by **Jayneen Sanders** illustrated by **Sofia Cardoso**

Teaching children about empathy, feelings, kindness, compassion, tolerance, respect and recognizing bullying behaviors

Dedication

For those adults who never hesitate to bend down, look
a child in the eyes, and say with empathy and kindness,
'I'm listening, I care and I understand.' JS

You, Me and Empathy
Educate2Empower Publishing an imprint of
UpLoad Publishing Pty Ltd
Victoria Australia
www.upload.com.au

First published in 2017

Text copyright © Jayneen Sanders 2017
Illustration copyright © Sofia Cardoso 2017

Written by Jayneen Sanders
Illustrations by Sofia Cardoso

Designed by Stephanie Spartels, Studio Spartels

National Library of Australia
Cataloguing-in-Publication Data

Creator: Sanders, Jayneen, author.

Title: You, me and empathy : teaching children about empathy, feelings, kindness, compassion, tolerance, respect and recognizing bullying behaviors / Jayneen Sanders ; illustrated by Sofia Cardoso.

ISBN: 9781925089080 (paperback)

Target Audience: For primary school age.

Subjects: Empathy--Juvenile fiction.
Kindness--Juvenile fiction
Children's stories.

Other Creators/Contributors: Cardoso, Sofia, illustrator.

you are
LOVED

Sometimes I feel just like you,
I understand what you're going through.
Sometimes you feel just like me.
That understanding is called empathy.
love
Quinn XX

When I was a baby, I really was small,
while everyone else seemed incredibly **tall**.

Family

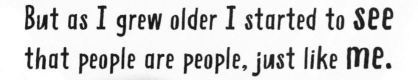

But as I grew older I started to **see** that people are people, just like **me.**

LAKE

How are you the same as your friend? Sister? Brother? How are you different?

Sometimes I'm *happy*

and sometimes I'm *sad,*

sometimes I'm *worried*

and sometimes I'm *mad.*

We all have feelings; you have them **too**,
and sometimes I feel just exactly like **you!**

What makes you happy?
Sad? Worried? Mad?

When my mother was sick with a tummy **bug**,
I knew that she needed a big snuggly **hug**.

I rubbed her back and patted her **hand,**
and said, "I'm so sorry; I do **understand.**"

9

For once I was sick with a terrible **flu**;
I sneezed and I spluttered but what could I **do?**
My mother said softly, while patting my **hand,**
"My dearest of dears, I do **understand.**"

That's when she gave me a big snuggly **hug**,
and I instantly knew I was humungously **loved**.
My mother was kind and caring to **me**;
exactly the same as how we should **be**.

Who helps you when you're sick?
How do they make you feel?

When my brother fell over and hurt his **knee**,
he cried and cried in front of **me.**

I helped him up and said, "There, **there**,"
and sat him down on the kitchen **chair.**

For once when I slipped and cut my **knee,**
my brother was there to care for **me.**

He held my hand and said, "There, **there,"**
and sat me down on the kitchen **chair.**

Who shows you kindness? In what
ways do they show you kindness?
How do you show kindness to others?

One day in the park, a girl was pushed **over**, knocked to the ground by a dog called **Rover**.

I knew his name, because, you see,
Rover the dog did the same thing to me!

The poor little girl sat still on the **ground**,
not a sob, not a whimper, not one little **sound**.
Then, all of sudden, she started to **cry**.
Perhaps I could help – it was worth a **try**.

"There, there," I said, as I patted her **arm**,
"Rover the dog doesn't mean any **harm**.
He's just being playful — so try not to **fuss**.
He just doesn't notice small people like **us!**"

Have you ever helped anyone
who was sad? How did you
help them?

One day at school while having **fun**,
I saw a boy alone in the **sun**.
No-one came over and said, "Let's **play**,"
I could see he was sad; he was not **okay**.

So I left my friends and over I **ran,**
and I asked if he'd like to play in the **sand.**
His smile was huge, enormous and **wide,**
it gave me a warm *fuzzy* feeling **inside.**

When I started school, I too sat **alone**.
I had no-one to play with; I longed to go **home**.
Then a girl called Abbey ran over to **me**
and asked me to play near the old oak **tree**.

We gathered some acorns for finger-hats,
and swung from the branches like acrobats.
We played for ages, and from that day,
"Friends forever!" we always say.

Have you got a good friend?
How does your friend make you feel?

Yesterday at the big green **slide**,
I saw a child run away and **hide**.
"Come back," said her dad. "Just give it a **try**.
This slide is not so terribly **high!**"

So up she climbed to the very top.
"Slide down," he said. "I'll help you to stop."
But there she sat and there she stayed,
wanting to move but too afraid.

I knew just how this girl was **feeling**;
worried and scared, her head was **reeling**;
for when I was little, I sat at the **top**,
terrified that I wouldn't **stop**.

"You CAN do this," is what I said.
"You're braver than you think, it's all in your head.
The more and more brave things you do,
the easier it becomes for you!"

"I **AM** really brave," the girl shouted **down.**

And **whooooooosssshhhh!**

Before we knew it, she was on the **ground!**

Have you ever felt scared?
What happened? Tell me about
a time you had to be brave.

There's one more story I'd like to **share**,
about a bully who never played **fair**.

He pushed children over, was mean and **unkind**.
He made us feel *sad*, so deep down **inside**.

But one day at school, I saw a strange **thing**;
the bully was bullied and pushed off a **swing.**
He was sad, he was crying as he walked **away.**
So I followed and asked him, "Are you **okay?**"

His eyes were watery, his nose was **red**,
he looked at me, these words he **said:**
"I was mean to the children, it just wasn't **right.**
I know how they feel now, I've had a big **fright.**
Kind and caring is how we should **be.**
I know this because a bully bullied **me!**"

Have you ever been bullied? How did it make you feel? What did you do?

So as I am growing taller each **day,**
I'm learning so much in so many **ways.**
I'm learning that we should try to be **kind,**
helpful and caring all of the **time.**

Our world is so special, we all need to **care** about one another and the earth we **share**. People together from far and from **wide**, we're all on this planet, we're on the same **side**.

COMMUNITY GARDEN

What might be some ways we could show other people we care about them?

So when someone's hurting or worried or **sad**,
remember those feelings I'm sure you've **had.**

Say kindly with care, "I understand – I do,
because sometimes I feel just exactly like you!"

Discussion Questions
for Parents, Caregivers and Educators

One of the most important social skills a child can learn is empathy. Being able to understand how another person is feeling and recognizing their needs helps people to connect to one another across race, culture and the diversity that is ever-present and so important to our world.

The following Discussion Questions are intended as a guide, and can be used to initiate an important dialogue with your child around empathy, feelings, kindness, compassion, tolerance, respect and recognizing bullying behaviors. The questions are optional and/or can be explored at different readings. I suggest you allow your child time to answer the questions both on the internal pages and in this section, as well as encouraging them to ask their own questions around this important topic.

Pages 4–5
Do you think babies know lots of things when they are born? Why do you say that? Do you think Quinn knows more things now that Quinn is older? Why do you say that? Do you know more things now that you are older? What kind of things do you know? What is different about the people in the picture (page 5)? What is the same?

Pages 6–7
When do you feel happy? Sad? Worried? Mad? Do you think other people have these kinds of feelings too? Why do you say that? How does it make you feel when you see that another person is sad? Happy? Worried? Mad?

Pages 8–9
What kind of person do you think Quinn is? How do you know? Do you think Quinn's mother likes to have Quinn beside her? Why do you say that?

Pages 10–11
Have you ever been sick with the flu? Who helped you? If your friend/brother/sister/mother/father was sick, what might you say or do to make them feel better?

Pages 12–13

When Quinn's brother fell over, how do you think Quinn knew what to do? What do you think Quinn's brother will do next to help Quinn? What would you do if your friend/brother/sister/mother/father fell over? How does it feel to help others? When you show kindness to someone, how do you think it makes that person feel?

Pages 14–15

How do you think the little girl is feeling? Have you ever been knocked over by a big dog/older person? How did you feel?

Pages 16–17

Why do you think Quinn offered to help? After Quinn spoke to the little girl, do you think she felt better? Why do you say that? Who else might be around to help this little girl? Do you like helping people? How does it make you feel?

Pages 18–19

How do you think the little boy is feeling? Have you ever felt lonely? What did you do? If you saw a lonely child in the playground, what would you do? Quinn was very kind. How do you think the boy felt when Quinn asked him to play? Why did Quinn have a warm fuzzy feeling inside?

Pages 20–21

When Quinn was lonely at school who showed Quinn kindness? What kind of person do you think Abbey is? Tell me all the things you really like about your good/best friend. What are the things your good/best friend likes about you?

Pages 22–23

How is this little girl feeling? Have you ever felt so scared you couldn't move? Tell me what happened. Did your body show any of your Early Warning Signs? (Note: read the children's book *My Body! What I Say Goes!* to learn about Early Warning Signs.) What do you think Quinn is thinking?

Pages 24–25

How did Quinn know just how the little girl was feeling? Do you think Quinn's words helped the little girl to be brave? Why do you say that?

Pages 26–27

How do you think the little girl is feeling now that she has gone down the slide? How do you think Quinn is feeling about helping the little girl?

Pages 28–29

How do you think the children on page 29 are feeling? What is Abbey doing?

Pages 30–31

Do you think the boy who was bullying the younger children has learned his lesson? Why do you say that?

Pages 32–33

Do you think our world is special? Why do you say that? How might we show people we care about them? Do we need to take care of the earth? Why do you say that?

How are the children in this picture the same? What does it mean, 'We're all on this planet, we're on the same side'?

Pages 34–35

What do you think has happened to Abbey? Do you think Quinn understands how Abbey is feeling? Why do you say that? What do you think 'empathy' means? That's right! It means we understand how another person is feeling because sometimes we feel that way too. Who are the people in your life who show you empathy and kindness? In what ways do they show you empathy and kindness? How do you show empathy and kindness to others (this can include animals)?

Suggested reading for adults: *Unselfie: Why Empathetic Kids Succeed in Our All-About-Me World* by Michele Borba, Ed. D; published by Touchstone.

Activities to Promote Empathy, Kindness and Compassion

'No act of kindness, no matter how small, is ever wasted.'
AESOP

Spare Change Jar: Have the family/class collect any spare change and place it in a jar. Decide where the money will go and label the jar. Ideas might be to a homeless shelter, Christmas Giving Tree, dog shelter and/or a local environmental group.

Friendship Seat: Have your children organize with their school/class a friendship seat. A child who has no-one to play with during recess, can sit on the friendship seat. When other children see the child sitting there, they can invite him or her to play with them, or they could spend some time sitting and talking with the child.

Shoe Swap: Have your child wear your shoes. Now have them express how it feels to be you! Lead them into imagining they are wearing another's shoes, for example, the shoes of an older relative, a younger cousin or a newly arrived immigrant. Discuss how life might be for that person.

Kind Deeds: Brainstorm and then list '10 Kind Deeds' your family/class could accomplish over the next twelve months. Tick them off as they occur.

Donate Old Clothes and Books: Invite your child to come with you when you donate their old clothes and books to a charity shop. Explain to them why it is important to recycle and re-use. Encourage your child to ask the volunteers about their work and why they volunteer.

Sister School: Encourage your child to ask their teacher if they can match up with a 'sister school'. Each child in the class can be allocated an 'email pal' from the sister school. Children are encouraged to ask questions of their email pals to find out how their lives are the same or different.

'Adopt' an Older Person: Have you family 'adopt' an older person in your neighborhood who may need help or is simply lonely. Ask them questions about their life and/or invite them to share photographs from the past. *Note: ensure your child is not left unaccompanied.*

Learn a Language: If there are children at your child's school who speak another language at home or you have refugees living nearby, encourage your child (and the whole family) to learn some basic greetings in that person's language. Chat to them in both your language and theirs about their country and welcome them by showing an interest in their culture.

Bake Something: As a family activity, bake some cookies or a meal for a person/s who is ill, sad, lonely, new to the neighborhood or just because you want to!

Write a Letter: Encourage your child to write a thank-you letter or an email to a person who has shown them kindness and/or whom they admire, stating the reasons why.

Asking Questions: Encourage your child to ask questions of others, for example, instead of talking about what they received for Christmas they might ask a friend/cousin/neighbor what they were given for Christmas instead. Remind your child everyone has a story and it is by asking questions we find out about each other.

Model Empathy and Kindness: Children learn through modeling. By helping that older neighbor mow their lawn or volunteering for the school fair or helping to collect left-over food for a homeless shelter you are modeling to children that you care.

Books by the Same Author

This beautifully illustrated children's picture book sensitively broaches the subject of safe and unsafe touch. This book will assist parents, carers and educators to broach this subject with children in a non-threatening and age-appropriate way. Discussion Questions included. **Ages 3 to 11 years.**

A story about an empowered little girl with a strong voice on all issues, especially those relating to her body! A book to teach children about personal boundaries, respect and consent; empowering children by respecting their choices and their right to say, 'No!' Discussion Questions included. **Ages 2 to 9 years.**

This beautifully illustrated children's book raises awareness around gender equality, respectful relationship, feelings, choice, self-esteem, tolerance and acceptance. In order to reduce gender-based violence, we need to teach children gender equality and respectful relationships from the earliest of years. Discussion Questions included. **Ages 2 to 9 years.**

Captain Pearl Fairweather is a brave, fair and strong pirate captain. She and her diverse crew of twenty-four women sail the seven seas on the good ship, Harmony, looking only for adventure. This beautifully illustrated book sets out to empower young girls to be strong, assertive and self-confident and for boys to respect, value and embrace that empowerment. Discussion Questions included. **Ages 5 to 12 years.**

An essential step-by-step guide for parents, carers and educators on how to protect children from sexual abuse. This guide contains simple, practical and age-appropriate ideas and activities, as well as important information for adults on grooming, signs of abuse and disclosure responses.

A children's picture book to empower and teach children about personal body safety, feelings, safe and unsafe touch, private parts, secrets and surprises, consent and respect. This book provides everything a child needs to know to help keep them safe from inappropriate touch. Discussion Questions included. **Ages 3 to 9 years.**

For more information go to: www.e2epublishing.info